THE THREE LITTLE WITCHES
STORYBOOK

'irresistible for newly fluent readers.'

Financial Times

'This quirky, beautifully illustrated storybook
is ideal for reading aloud and sharing with young children.'

Book Trusted News

'an excellent book to read aloud.'

Glasgow Herald

'This lovely story book is instantly appealing.
Beautifully illustrated in gorgeous colours …
The exuberant illustrations burst from the page,
adding immeasurably to the lively text.
An ideal book to read aloud.'

Armadillo

THE
THREE LITTLE
WITCHES
STORYBOOK

I'm Ziggy

GEORGIE ADAMS AND EMILY BOLAM

Dolphin

First published in 2001 by
Orion Children's Books
This edition published 2003 by Dolphin paperbacks
a division of the Orion Publishing Group Ltd
Orion House
5 Upper St Martin's Lane
London   WC2H 9EA

Text copyright © Georgie Adams 2001
Illustrations copyright © Emily Bolam 2001
Designed by Tracey Cunnell

A catalogue record for this book is available from the British Library
Printed and bound in Italy
ISBN I 84255 074 8

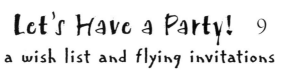

CONTENTS

Let's Have a Party!

Once upon a time there were three little witches called Zara, Ziggy and Zoe.

Zara had a frog called Fidget.	Ziggy had a cat called Jelly.	Zoe had an owl called Two Hoots.

They all lived together in Cauldron Cottage, deep in Magic Wood.

One morning while they were having breakfast the calendar on the wall flipped over a page and sang a little song.

TODAY'S BEGUN, THE NIGHT HAS BEEN—
NOT LONG, I SEE, TILL HALLOWE'EN!

Ugh!
Frog flakes!

FROSTED
FROG
FLAKES

"Hickety-pickety," said Zara, crunching her frosted frog flakes. "It's nearly the end of October already."

"Hinks-minx," said Ziggy, munching her crispy cracklers. "I love Hallowe'en!"

"Wippety-woppet," said Zoe, swallowing a mouthful of magic milkshake. It fizzed and tickled her tongue. "Let's have a party!"

"Then we could dress up and look spooky!" said Ziggy.

Whoo! Hoo!

Scary!

"A party *would* be fun," said Zara. "Let's do it. We can send out the invitations today."

So the three little witches made a wish list of everyone they wanted to ask to their party. Zoe wrote it down with her special pen and magic ink. It was the sort that turned a different colour for every letter. It made splodges on words it didn't like.

"Wizard Wink," said Zara.

"Baby Dragon," said Ziggy.

"Tag, Tig and Tog Troll," said Zoe.

"Max and Mick," said Ziggy.

"Those wizard boys had better behave," said Zara. "Remember when they put a spell on my broomstick? I was flying upside down for a whole week."

Ziggy and Zoe got the giggles. But they stopped giggling when Zara said:

"What about Melissa?"

Zoe wrote down Melissa's name.

"Oh, not that horrid little witch!" said Ziggy.

"Remember when she turned Jelly into a frog like Fidget?"

I remember it well!

You looked great as a frog!

Zoe crossed Melissa's name out. At once slime green ink burst out of the pen and splattered all over the page.

"It's a sign. She knows you've crossed her out!" cried Zara. "Put her back or there'll be trouble!"

So Zoe wrote down Melissa's name again. It looked rather messy. The pen didn't like writing *her* name one little bit.

"That's enough," said Zara. "How many are there?"
The names on the list shouted out their numbers.

Then Max and Mick started arguing because Melissa had pushed in front and made herself number six. They couldn't agree who was seven and who was eight.

"Oh, stop it," said Zara. "I'll count you myself."

When she had finished the three little witches got busy and wrote out all the invitations. They did their very best writing and tried not to make any spelling mistakes.

The invitations looked like this.

COME TO OUR
PARTY!

at Midnight

on Hallowe'en

Tricks, treats and monster jelly!

Please reply to:

Zara, Ziggy and Zoe

Cauldron Cottage

Magic Wood

Then they addressed the envelopes like this.

Wizard Wink
The School House
Magic Wood

Baby Dragon
Mountain Cave
Magic Wood

Max and Mick
The Tree House
Leapfrog Lane
Magic Wood

Tag, Tig and Tog
Bridge End
Magic Wood

That looks a mess!

Melissa
The Webs
Which Way
Magic Wood

Melissa's envelope was a bit splodgy.

Next Zara tapped the pile of invitations with her finger and chanted a spell:

HURRY NOW TO HOUSE AND DEN
AND BRING THE ANSWERS BACK AGAIN!

I can't wait for them all to reply.

I wonder who'll be first?

We'll just have to wait and see!

And at once each invitation sprouted tiny wings and fluttered off to deliver itself to someone in Magic Wood.

Zoe's Tidy Spell

The little witches liked living in Cauldron Cottage.

Downstairs there was:

a den for games

a place to keep their broomsticks

a sitting room where they watched television

a kitchen

Upstairs there was:

a bathroom

three little bedrooms

ZARA'S ROOM

ZIGGY'S ROOM

BEWARE SPELLS

ZOE'S ROOM

Zara, Ziggy and Zoe each had their own room, with their name on the door.

One morning the little witches were busy doing housework.
There was lots to do so they used some magic to help them.
They chanted:

BROOM, BROOM, SWEEP THE FLOOR.
DUSTER DUST THE SHELVES.
CUPS AND PLATES JUMP INTO THE BOWL –
AND WASH UP BY YOURSELVES!

But this morning some of the magic went wrong.

In the kitchen Milk Jug
squeezed too much
washing-up liquid
into the bowl.

SQUEEESH!

SQUOOOS

SCARY LIQUID

The Taps turned themselves
FULL ON and squirted
soapy water everywhere!

Hic!

Hic!

Hic!

The Teacups thought it was
very funny. They laughed so
much, they got H^{I}C$_C$U^{P}S.

Ping!

POP!

As for the Spoons, they
had a lovely time playing
with the bubbles.

The little witches found the kitchen floor covered in foam.
"Hinks-minx!" cried Ziggy. "That spell went wonky."
But it was fun to play for a while.

Then they mopped up the mess.

This looks like trouble. I'm off!

Afterwards Zoe went upstairs with Two Hoots to tidy her room.

"Where shall I start?" she said.

"Over here!" said Bed.

"Under here!" said Shoes.

"On here!" said Desk.

"Behind here!" said Socks.

"In here!" said Cupboard.

Zoe's spell book must be here somewhere!

In here!

On here!

Behind here!

Zoe sat on her bed. She had lost her Spell Book *again* and was trying to remember the spell for putting things away.

She closed her eyes and began like this:

'TIDDLE-TUM TAY. MUDDLE WHIRL AWAY . . .'

But before she could think of the next line a mighty gust of wind blew her bedroom window open.

BANG!

Over here!

Under here!

Zoe jumped with surprise. Her words had called up a twirly-whirly wind by mistake!

WHOOOOOOOOOOOO!

It whisked around the room and sent things flying.

WHOOOOOOOOOOOOO!

Her bed flew up to the ceiling.
"Wippety-woppet!" she cried.
Zoe's things whizzed about faster and faster.

I think Zoe got that spell wrong somehow!

WHOOOOOOOOOOO!

27

Luckily the spell soon wore off and the twirly-whirly wind went away. Zoe's bed crashed to the floor.

"My room looks worse than ever, now!" cried Zoe. "I WISH I could remember that tidy spell . . ."

Just then Zoe's missing Spell Book landed on the bed with a THUMP!

"Wowee!" she said. "Now I can do the spell."

"Tidy spell. Page forty-two," said Spell Book, flipping through his pages. "You really should know it by now."

Bossy old thing! thought Zoe. But she WAS glad to see him.

"I'll read it," said Spell Book.

"Thank you," said Zoe.

So he read the spell out loud:

TIDDLE-TUM TAY. MUDDLE WHIRL AWAY.
BIM-BAM-BOOM. TIDY UP THIS ROOM!

Spell Book shouted the last words, then slammed himself shut.

And this time the spell worked like magic.

That's much better!

Zara and Ziggy came to look at Zoe's tidy room. They had been busy too.

"I've dusted my frog collection," said Zara.

She nearly dusted ME!

"I've made my bed PROPERLY," said Ziggy. "It took me ages."

Good! Now I can sleep on it.

At last the little witches finished doing their jobs. They sat down for a drink of lemonade and blew bubbles through their straws.

Suddenly the television switched itself on.

"Time for telly!" it cried.

So the little witches sat down to watch their favourite TV programme — *Weenie the Wonderwitch!* Zara, Ziggy and Zoe loved Weenie — her spells were always going wrong.

You'd have thought they'd had enough wonky magic for one day, wouldn't you?

Time for telly!

crow mail

Remember those party invitations?
The very FIRST reply arrived by special Crow delivery!
The little witches were very excited.

Zara opened the envelope.

Then she read the letter
to Ziggy and Zoe.

Special Delivery –
as the crow flies

To Littel Witchiz
Call Dron Cottage
Magic Wood

crow mail

"Max and Mick
are coming!" said
Zara. "I wonder
who'll be next?"

Dear Zara ~~Piggy~~ Ziggy Zoeee

Thanks for yor IN VIT A SHUN.
Cool! We will bee there.
From Max and Mick
P.S. We promiss not two
do any bad trix.

This is a pick ~~tuer~~
of oUr Tree House.
Hope you like it!

Wizard Wink's school

The little witches go to Wizard Wink's school in Magic Wood. They learn to read and write. And they have special lessons in magic as well!

One morning while the little witches were having breakfast the kitchen clock sang out the time:

**HURRY, HURRY, DON'T BE LATE—
OFF TO SCHOOL, IT'S HALF-PAST EIGHT!**

"Wippety-woppet!" spluttered Zoe through a spoonful of cacklepops. "I wonder where we'll find it today?"

Wizard Wink's school was magic. It had a habit of running away. The little witches were used to finding it in a new place every day.

"It could be *anywhere*," said Ziggy, gulping down her milkshake.

"We'll ask Signpost," said Zara, licking jellyfish jam from her fingers. "Race you to the crossroads!"

Here we go again!

33

So the little witches raced off and Zara got there first.
"Please Signpost, have you seen our school?" she asked.
"Now, let me think . . ." he said. "Ah, yes! It ran by
a moment ago. It went puffing down Leapfrog Lane.
You'll catch it, if you hurry."

OTHER WAY

THAT WAY

THIS WAY

WHICH WAY

LANE

It's all right
for you. I
have to HOP!

Rush, rush,
rush.

"Thank you, Signpost!" said the little witches, and they hurried on. They soon found the school. It had stopped by the stream for the day. Wizard Wink was waiting for them by the door.

"Come along," he said. "You're just in time."

Big Red Book called out the names of everyone in class:

"Tag!" "Tig!" "Tog!" "Baby Dragon!" "Mick

"Max!" "Melissa!" "Zoe!" "Ziggy!" "Zara!"

INK

"Ten names. Ten ticks. Everyone's here today!" said Big Red Book.

What about us?

We're here too!

We should be in Big Red Book.

36

"Good," said Wizard Wink. "We'll start with Numbers."

"Oh no!" groaned Max and Mick.

The wizard boys didn't like school much. They wanted to play. Wizard Wink asked them the first question.

"If I had three crystal balls in one hand . . ." he said, "and four in the other . . . what would I have?"

"BIG HANDS!" shouted Max and Mick.

"Very funny," said Wizard Wink.

"Oooh! I know. I know!" said Zoe. "Seven!"

"Right!" said Wizard Wink.

"Poo!" said Melissa. "That was easy-peasy."

That was quick!

But it wasn't easy!

"Well Melissa," said Wizard Wink, "can you tell me how many beans make five?"

Melissa didn't know the answer.

But Zara did.

"Five beans make five!" she said.

Amazing!

Melissa was very cross. Zara and Zoe were always getting their answers right. And she always got hers wrong. It wasn't fair!

So she decided to play a rotten trick on them. Melissa waited until breaktime while everyone was drinking Funfizz. It tasted of any flavour you wished for. Melissa looked at Zoe and Zara's drinks and whispered:

IZZ, WHIZZ, FUNFIZZ!

And she wished it tasted of slugs.
It was disgusting.

I like slugs!

Flies are my favourite.

So Zoe and Zara wished Melissa's drink tasted of bad eggs.
That was much worse!

Poo! Bad eggs. What a pong!

After break they did some painting. Everyone loved this lesson – even the wizard boys! Wizard Wink gave the class *magic* paints to make their pictures come alive – like these:

HALLOWE'EN PARTY
by Zoe

MAGIC CAULDRON
by Ziggy

FROGS
by Zara

I wonder what's brewing?

This one looks just like me!

A WICKED WOLF
by Melissa

FIREWORKS
by Baby Dragon

MONSTERS
by Mick and Max

DIGGING FOR GOLD
by Tag, Tig and Tog

 ~ Spooky!

The lesson was going well until . . .

Ziggy's cauldron overflowed . . .
the wicked wolf chased Zara's frogs . . .
the monsters messed up Zoe's party . . .
and Baby Dragon's rocket went WHIZZ! BANG!
all round the classroom.

WHIZZ! BANG!

Phew! That rocket
just missed me.

Help!

CROAK!
Nice wolfy!

Wizard Wink had to wave his wand to put things RIGHT.

The last lesson was writing. Wizard Wink told everyone he was going to write something for them to copy. He muttered a spell and these words appeared on the board like magic:

It looks like frog writing.

IF YOU CAN READ THIS
YOU ARE VERY CLEVER!

Ha ha.

The little witches copied it neatly in their writing books.
Then Wizard Wink said,
    "Who can tell me what it says?"
    "I CAN!" said Zoe.

If you can read this you are very clever!

IF YOU CAN READ THIS YOU ARE VERY CLEVER!

What a clever little witch!

The secret is to read the strange-looking words in a MIRROR – just like Zoe is doing!
    "Well done!" said Wizard Wink.
    And he gave her a smily star.

"Now," said Wizard Wink, "there's just time for me to show you a new spell before you go home."

Everyone crowded round to watch as he chanted these words:

SLIMY FROGSPAWN, SLIPPERY SNAILS
MIX TOGETHER WITH LIZARD TAILS
TOE OF TOAD, EYE OF NEWT
BREW IT UP IN A SMELLY OLD BOOT!

"What's the spell for?" asked Zoe.

"I'll show you," said Wizard Wink.

"And me!" said Melissa.

"And us!" said the trolls.

"Let's see!" said the wizard boys.

"And me!" said Baby Dragon.

"I'll show ALL OF YOU!" said Wizard Wink.

He stirred the mixture with his wand and gave everyone a drop. And this is what happened.

I've SHRUNK.

I'm as small as Fidget.

I'm as tiny as a teaspoon.

Crazy!

Hi!

Well, stand still and don't stir!

44

Everyone thought it was great fun.

Wizard Wink didn't let them stay like that for long. He waved his wand and everyone grew again.

"Now," he said, "it's time to go home. I'll see you all tomorrow."

The crow brought the SECOND reply in a packet.
It looked like this.

★ ★ ★ ★ ★ ★ ★ ★

Instant Star Signs

★ ★ ★ ★ ★ ★ ★

The brighter way
to send your message!
Just add water

★ ★ ★ ★ ★ ★ ★ ★

Ziggy read the
instructions on the back.

Instructions

★ ★ ★ ★ ★ ★ ★ ★

READ CAREFULLY
BEFORE OPENING.
1. Open packet.
2. Pour Instant Star Signs
powder into bowl.
3. Add water
4. Stand clear to read message!

★ ★ ★ ★ ★ ★ ★ ★

So Ziggy followed the
instructions and this
is what happened.

To
Zara
Ziggy
Zoe
I'm
coming
so there!
Melissa

"I thought Melissa would come!" said Ziggy.
"Max, Mick and Melissa," said Zara. "That's three."
"I wonder who'll be next?" said Zoe.

46

Zara Cooks a Treat

One afternoon Zara put on her apron and took her magic Cookery Book off the shelf. She was going to make something special for tea. She tapped Cookery Book and said:

SAUSAGES IN BATTER!

At once Cookery Book opened himself at the right page. Next he called out all the things she would need:

The things jumped on to the table as soon as their names were called.

Cookery Book sang out the
word Toads very loudly and
chuckled. He said it again
and again just for fun.

Toads

Toads

TOADS!

"Hickety-pickety!" said Zara.
"You know you should have said SAUSAGES – not Toads."

But it was too late. Fat lumpy toads had appeared in the kitchen.
They were all over the floor.

Zara was wondering how to get rid of them when Jelly came in.

Missed him
by a whisker!

Let's
hop it!

That was
close.

The toads hopped away as fast as they could, with Jelly close
behind. Zara shut Cookery Book before he could cause any more
trouble.

48

Then she snapped her fingers and chanted a spell:

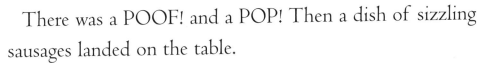

SPLITTER, SPLITTER, SPLATTER
SAUSAGES AND BATTER.
BAKE THEM IN A DISH FOR TEA
FOR ZIGGY AND ZOE AND ME!

There was a POOF! and a POP! Then a dish of sizzling sausages landed on the table.

At that moment Ziggy and Zoe came in.

"Tea's ready," said Zara.

"Brill!" said Ziggy.

"Wicked!" said Zoe.

So the little witches sat down to eat. As for those toads . . . they were croaking happily outside.

It wasn't long before the THIRD reply arrived.
The crow brought the little witches a note burnt with fire.

"I think I know who this is from!" said Zoe.

Dear little witches
Thank you very much
for your invitation.
I can come.
Lots of love
Baby Dragon
× × × × × × ×

crow mail

"How many are coming now?" said Zara.

"Max, Mick, Melissa and Baby Dragon," said Zoe.

"That's four," said Ziggy. "I can't wait to see who's next!"

Ziggy's New Broomstick

One day while Ziggy was out flying, her broomstick went
CRACK!

"Hinks-minx!" she cried as the stick broke in two.

A few seconds later,

THUMP! BUMP! Ziggy and Jelly crash-landed in Magic Wood.

"It's time I had a new broomstick," said Ziggy, rubbing her knee.

And they walked home.

It's time I stopped flying!

When they were back at Cauldron Cottage, there was a knock at the door. It was a goblin.

"Broomsticks for sale!" said the goblin.

"Ooh, just what I wanted!" said Ziggy.

It didn't take Ziggy long to choose the one she wanted.

"The best!" said the goblin.

The label on the box read:

I don't like the look of any of them.

The BEST!

You mean the worst

So Ziggy bought the broomstick. She paid the goblin ten quibs and fifty tots in witch money. It looked like this.

"Thank you!" said the goblin. "Happy flying!"

And he went away.

Ziggy took her new broomstick outside. She couldn't wait to try it.

Just then Max and Mick swooped down on their broomsticks. The wizard boys had spotted the Comet and wanted a closer look.

"Cool," said Max.

"Bet it *goes!*" said Mick.

"I'll race you!" said Ziggy.

I was afraid you'd say that.

"Great idea! Let's fly three times round Magic Wood," said Mick.

"First one back here is the winner!" said Max.

Ziggy put Jelly on the broomstick and climbed on. They all waited while Jelly got her balance. She wibbled and wobbled and clutched the twigs with her claws.

"She'll never stay on," said Max.

"She needs some glue," joked Mick.

When she was ready, Ziggy started the race like this.

"One . . . two . . . three . . . UP!" she cried.

They all tapped their broomsticks, and then they were off.

Wow wheeee!

Oops!
I'll never
stay on
this thing.

Ziggy's new broomstick shot up SO fast her tummy did a
somersault!

"Wow wheeee!" she went.

Poor Jelly shut her eyes and clung on.

Ziggy pushed the stick down a bit and the Comet zoomed
forward. Max and Mick chased her. The wind nearly blew their
hats off as they sped along, trying to keep up. But Ziggy raced
ahead once, twice round Magic Wood.

"That broomstick's a whizzer," shouted Max as they went round
for the third time.

"Let's slow it down," said Mick.

They waved their wands at Ziggy's broomstick . . .
and it began to behave very strangely.

It shook,

flew sideways,

dived,

and did a loop-the-loop!

This is
the end!

Ziggy and Jelly nearly fell off!

Ziggy was struggling to control the
broomstick as the wizard boys flew by.

"Having trouble?" shouted Max.

"Sorry, can't stop. We're in a race!" called Mick.

Ziggy guessed they had cheated by using magic. As soon as
her broomstick was flying properly again, she did some magic
of her own. I'll teach them to play tricks on me! she thought.

By this time Max and Mick were almost back at Cauldron
Cottage. The wizard boys were sure they would win the race.
Ziggy was nowhere to be seen! They flew over the signpost . . .
swerved right, then left . . . just a few trees to go . . .

Suddenly they looked down and saw a tree. It was a very odd one.
It had sweets all over it.

Max and Mick loved sweets!
But they had never seen a
sweetie tree before.

"Yahoo!" went Max.

"Here we come!" cried Mick.

They thought they could
stop for a while – and STILL
win the race. So they flew
down. But once they started
eating the sweets – they were
Ziggy's *magic* sweets –

THEY COULD NOT STOP!

Greedily they crammed lollipops,
toffees, chews and chocolate drops
into their mouths. Their cheeks
were bulging with sticky things.
When they had picked all the
sweets from the lower branches,
they climbed the tree for more.

It wasn't long before Ziggy flew over her magic tree. She waved to them and called out,

"Can't stop. I'm in a race!"

"THE RACE!" groaned the wizard boys.

Max and Mick had been so busy eating sweets they had forgotten all about it. Now they were feeling too sick to bother.

So Ziggy swooshed on to Cauldron Cottage and won the race after all.

"Tricks or no tricks," Ziggy told Jelly at bedtime that night, "I think my new broomstick's GREAT!"

But Jelly was sound asleep.

She'd had enough flying for a very long time!

The FOURTH reply was a Spell-o-gram. One afternoon it fluttered in through an open window.

Spell-o-gram

To Zara, Ziggy and Zoe

Cauldron Cottage, Magic Wood

Thank you

for your invitation. I should love to

come to your party

From Wizard Wink

Zara, Ziggy and Zoe read the Spell-o-gram.

"How many is that now?" said Zara.

"Max, Mick, Melissa, Baby Dragon and Wizard Wink," said Ziggy. "That's five."

"Who else?" said Zoe.

"The trolls," said Zara. "I hope they can come!"

shooting star Magic

One starry evening the little witches were having fun in Magic Wood. They were playing hide-and-seek with Baby Dragon and the trolls, Tag, Tig and Tog.

When it was Ziggy's turn to count, the others went to hide.

"One . . . two . . . three . . ." she began.

And a little later,

"Ninety-eight, ninety-nine, ONE HUNDRED. Coming!"

Ziggy searched around for them.

She found Zara here.

She saw Zoe there.

Finding Baby Dragon was easy. His flames gave him away.

But she couldn't find Tag, Tig or Tog anywhere. They had disappeared.

Zara, Ziggy and Zoe wondered where the trolls could be.

Suddenly there was a loud swishing noise overhead.

SWOOOOOSH!

A tiny golden star came shooting from the sky. It showered them with sparks.

"Oooh!" sighed Baby Dragon. He loved fiery things.

"Look, it went over there!" said Zoe.

"Let's go and find it," said Zara.

"And keep a lookout for those trolls!" said Ziggy.

They're nuts!

SWOOOOOSH!

The sky's falling down!

Take cover!

Tag, Tig and Tog had forgotten all about playing hide-and seek. Trolls are *very* forgetful! Instead of hiding, they had gone to dig for treasure.

They were working away when the star came down. It landed right where they were digging. They thought they had found a shiny nugget of gold.

"Gold!" said Tag.
"Treasure!" said Tig.
"We're rich!" said Tog.
"That's MINE!" said somebody else.

It was that meanie witch Melissa who was hiding nearby. She had mistaken the star for gold too. Melissa wanted the treasure for herself.

"Give me the gold or you'll be sorry," she said, suddenly jumping out at them.

"But it's ours," said Tag.

"We found it!" said Tig.

"So PUSH OFF!" said Tog.

"I warned you," said Melissa, opening a packet of magic powder, "if you don't give me the gold I'll turn you hairy little trolls into toadstools! Ha, ha, ha!"

And she threw some powder at the trolls . . .

Just then the little witches and Baby Dragon came along. The powder made Baby Dragon SNEEZE.

AH-TISHOO! AAH-TISHOO! AAAH-TISHOO

It's very windy round here!

The last and BIGGEST sneeze blew the magic powder all over Melissa. Then she looked like a toadstool.

The little witches had a fit of the giggles.

The trolls fell about laughing.

"Tee, hee, hee! Melissa's a toadstool!" they shrieked.

Baby Dragon looked worried.

"Melissa will say it's all my fault," he said. "When the magic wears off I'll be in BIG trouble!"

AAAAH-TISHOOO!

The little witches started whispering to each other. They had an idea.

Hopping mad, I'd say!

She doesn't look too pleased about it.

Zara picked up the star. It glistened with stardust. Ziggy chanted a spell and Zoe blew stardust over the toadstool. *POOF!*

It fizzed and sparkled like a firework.

"Melissa will forget all about this when she changes back again," said Zara. "The magic will soon wear off and she won't remember anything!"

Baby Dragon WAS pleased. He thanked the little witches like this:

Thankyou very much little witches

Afterwards the trolls picked up the star. It looked very ordinary without its stardust. It was just a lump of old rock.

"It's not shining any more," said Tag.

"Or glittering," said Tig.

"It isn't gold, after all," said Tog.

"Never mind," said Ziggy. "The star DID help us with that spell."

Then the little witches, Baby Dragon and the trolls all went home to bed.

Later when the magic wore off and Melissa changed back from being a toadstool . . . she didn't remember a THING!

At last the Crow brought the FIFTH reply to the little witches.
It was a magic postcard from Bridge End.

Ziggy thanked the Crow and looked at it.

GREETINGS from Bridge End

POST CARD

Dear little Witches,
Thank you for your invitation. We will be there on the stroke of Midnight!

Tag, Tig and Tog
× × ×

To Zara, Ziggy and Zoe
Cauldron Cottage
Magic Wood

"It's from Tag, Tig and Tog," she said.

"Let's see," said Zoe.

"Are they coming?" said Zara.

Ziggy turned the postcard over and read it out loud.

"Yes!" she cried. "The trolls ARE coming!"

shopping at Whizzo's

It was the day before Hallowe'en. The little witches were on their way to Whizzo's supermarket to buy things for the party. At the crossroads they met their friend Signpost.

"Which way to Whizzo's today?" said Zara.

"That depends which day it *is*," said Signpost.

"It's Friday," said Zoe.

"Ah!" said Signpost, waving his arms about. "If it's Friday . . . go THAT way."

He pointed to a path between the trees.

I'm confused.

Me too.

"If you had been here yesterday," he went on, "you would have gone THIS way. It was the OTHER way last Monday . . . or was it Tuesday?"

The little witches were getting muddled.

"Thank you," said Ziggy. "We'll try THAT way. I'm sure you're right."

"Half left, half right," said Signpost. "Goodbye."

The little witches hurried along the path. It *was* the right one, and soon they reached the supermarket. They took a shopping trolley and went inside.

WHIZZO'S

EVERYTHING A WITCH COULD WANT!

Whizzo's sold everything a little witch could want. First they went by shelves full of things for making spells.

SPELL MAKING

WORM JUICE WORM JUICE WORM JUICE WORM JUICE WORM JUICE WORM JUICE WORM JUICE

Lizard legs   Lizard legs   Lizard legs

SUN-DRIED BONES

FREE RANGE DRAGON EGGS

RATS   RATS   RATS   RATS

PICKLED BEAKS

SPECIAL MOONWEED

Delicious!

WORM JUICE

Then they stopped to look at some magic books and saw Wizard Wink. Their teacher was very clever – he wrote lots of books! Wizard Wink was selling copies of his latest bestspelling book *Spellbound*. So the little witches bought a copy. They paid him five quibs and ten tots.

Wizard Wink signed it for them. He wrote inside:

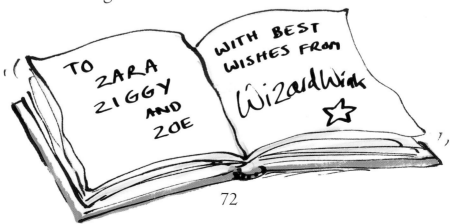

At last they found what they were looking for
and bought things for the party:

Hallowe'en Fun

They look good!

They look scary!

I'm n-n-not s-c-a-r-e-d of g-g-ghosts!

By now their trolley was nearly full. But there was enough room
for some sweets. So they bought some jelly beans, dragon drops
and fizzy sherbet bugs.

Suddenly Zoe gave a shout.

"Look out!" she cried.

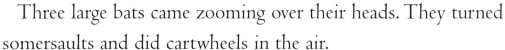

I wish I could do tha[t]

Three large bats came zooming over their heads. They turned somersaults and did cartwheels in the air.

"Amazing!" said Ziggy.

"Let's buy them," said Zoe.

"Yes, let's!" said Zara.

But catching them wasn't easy . . .

Phew!

Phew!

Zara raced around and caught one beside the crystal balls.

Zoe climbed over some cauldrons and got another.

And Ziggy went skidding into a pile of pumpkins . . . and grabbed the last one!

Run for it!

PHEW! went the witches.

Z-Z-Z-Z-Z-Z-z-z-z- went the bats. They were so tired after all that flying . . . they folded their wings and went to sleep!

"Let's get them home before they wake up!" said Zara.

So the little witches hurried to the checkout.

"Bats are on Special Offer this week," said the goblin at the till. "Buy two – get one FREE."

He added up the bill.

"That'll be sixty-two quibs and twenty tots," he said.

The little witches paid the goblin, put the bats into carrying boxes and staggered out with their bags.

"What a whopping lot of shopping!" said Ziggy.

That night the little witches spent a long time watching the bats.
They could do fantastic flying tricks . . .

wing to wing

upside down

and backwards!

They're great
acroBATS!

Brill for
the party!

I can't wait for
tomorrow night!

Before they went to bed the little witches looked at all the replies and counted up.

And Jelly and Fidget and me make fourteen!

"Max, Mick, Melissa, Baby Dragon, Wizard Wink, Tag, Tig and Tog."

"Eight!" said Zoe.

"And US!" said Zara.

"Eleven!" said Ziggy.

"ZICKERY, ZACKERY, DOODLE-DO!"

Party Night!

It was the day of the little witches' party! Zara, Ziggy and Zoe were busy getting things ready. The calendar on the kitchen wall was very cheerful today. It sang over and over again:

THE LAST DAY OF OCTOBER—
OCTOBER THIRTY-ONE.
HALLOWE'EN IS HERE AT LAST,
IT'S TIME TO HAVE SOME FUN!

The little witches sang along as they made crazy food for their party.

Cookery Book flipped his pages and called out recipes for:

Fudge feet!

Witchy fingers!

Toothy bites!

Bat cakes!

Monster jellies!

Beetleburgers!

They also put some laughing sweets in a dish.

Afterwards they did the decorations.
Ziggy blew up balloons.
Zara sat the skeleton in a corner.
Zoe dangled spiders in the windows.

I wish they were REAL.

Whoooo-arrh!

Then the little witches stopped for a rest.
"It looks really spooky," said Zara.
"*Whoooo-arrh!*" moaned Ziggy.
"I wish it was midnight now!" said Zoe.

Can you hop?

Zara looked outside. It was getting dark.
"Time to make the lanterns," she said.
So they each took a pumpkin and put a candle inside
to make a lantern.
Then they lit the candles carefully and hung
the lanterns outside, by the door.
The pumpkins glowed in the dark.

**ELEVEN O'CLOCK, I KNOW THAT'S RIGHT—
ONE HOUR TO GO BEFORE . . . MIDNIGHT!**

sang the clock.

"Hickety-pickety," said Zara.

"Have we got everything ready?" said Zoe.

"Everything except . . . US," said Ziggy.

So the little witches dressed up in their very best Hallowe'en outfits.

And just before TWELVE o'clock, they counted down the seconds:

Five! Four! Three! Two! ONE!

Freaky!

Wild!

Weird!

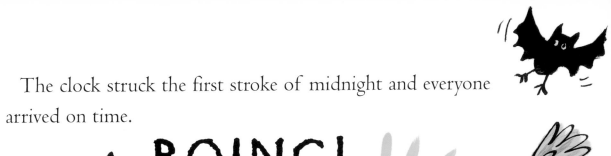

The clock struck the first stroke of midnight and everyone arrived on time.

BOING!

First they played Spot-the-Spook. Everyone hunted for the ghost the little witches had bought at Whizzo's.

W HOOooo-ARRH-OOOooo

The ghost drifted about,

WHOOooo-ARRH-OOOooo

popped up in strange places,

WHOOooo-ARRH-OOOooo

grinned ghoulishly

and gave them all a fright . .

until it discovered the dish of laughing sweets the little witches had left on the table.

After that it went:

OOO-hoo-hoo-hoo-HA-HA-HA!

so loudly everyone knew where it was!

Next Wizard Wink had a surprise for the little witches.
He waved his wand and three pairs of silver boots appeared.
"Try them on," he said to Zara, Ziggy and Zoe.
So the little witches pulled them on.
"Now take a step," said the wizard, smiling mysteriously.
They each took one small step and . . .

POOF! PUFF! PING!

The little witches vanished.
"Brill!" said Ziggy.
"Wicked!" said Zoe.
"Magic!" said Zara.
They could be heard but not seen.

"I thought you'd like them," said Wizard Wink.

The little witches took the boots off and – *PING!* They were back again.

Melissa looked at the boots jealously. She wanted a pair for herself. So later, when she thought no one was looking, she quickly put one pair on.

BUT she was in such a hurry, she put the boots on the WRONG FEET. And this is what happened.

HELP!

She grew taller,   and taller,   and TALLER

until her head reached the ceiling.

"Help!" cried Melissa from a long way up.

"Dear me," said Wizard Wink, chuckling to himself.
Then he said a magic word.

SHOOLUM-BOOLUM-BOOTS UNDOODLE-UM!

And Melissa was the right size again.
"Silly old boots!" said Melissa, tugging them off.
"And NOW it's time to EAT!" said Zara.
She snapped her fingers and . . .

the toothy bites
gnashed their teeth,

the witchy fingers
beckoned spookily,

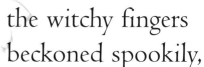

the monster jellies
waddled,

the fudge feet danced,

the beetleburgers scuttled about

and the bat cakes flew round the room.

Catching and eating them was the best fun of all.

Jelly, Fidget and Two Hoots joined in too.

And so did the three bats from Whizzo's. They tried some amazing flying tricks—with the bat cakes!

At last, when it was time to go home, everyone thanked the little witches for a lovely party. Even Melissa said she'd enjoyed herself – apart from that funny business with the boots! They all agreed it had been the best Hallowe'en they could remember for a long time.

And that night three tired but happy little witches flopped on the floor and yawned. It was time for bed.

So now we must leave them and say:

"Goodnight Zara."　　"Goodnight Ziggy."　　"Goodnight Zoe."

Goodnight little witches.

Goodnight!

WOOD

MOUNTAINS

MOUNTAIN CAVE
where Baby Dragon
lives

CAULDRON
COTTAGE

ere Zara, Ziggy
and Zoe live

where the shooting
star fell

BRIDGE END
where Tag, Tig
and Tog live

THE TREE HOUSE
where Mick and
Max live

KEEP
OUT!

where the
school ran to
one day

3

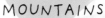